Dirty Bertie

Bertie

GERMS!

For Sam, who I'm sure would love
"The Dead Skunks" ~ D R
For Ella – Bertie's no. 1 fan ~ A M

STRIPES PUBLISHING LIMITED
An imprint of the Little Tiger Group
1 Coda Studios, 189 Munster Road,
London SW6 6AW

A paperback original
First published in Great Britain in 2009

Characters created by David Roberts
Text copyright © Alan MacDonald, 2009
Illustrations copyright © David Roberts, 2009

ISBN: 978-1-84715-073-8

Dirty Bertie

GERMS!

DAVID ROBERTS WRITTEN BY ALAN MACDONALD

Dirty Bertie
Collect all the
Dirty Bertie books!

Contents

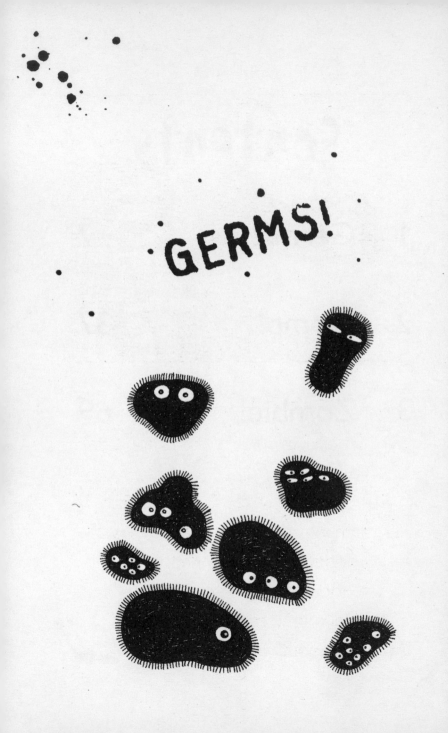

CHAPTER 1

"Are you all right?" said Mum. "You don't look well."

Bertie looked up from his breakfast. His mum was talking to Suzy, who had just drooped into the kitchen.

"I'm hot," she moaned.

"Actually I'm a bit hot," said Bertie, through a mouthful of cereal.

"My head aches," croaked Suzy. "I ache all over."

"My head's sort of achey," said Bertie. "It aches when I talk."

Mum paid no attention. "Let me look at you," she said to Suzy. "Goodness! Look at these spots! I think you've got chickenpox."

"Chickenpox?" groaned Suzy.

"Chickenpox!" said Bertie.

Mum fetched her big blue medical book and turned the pages. "Here it is," she said. "Chickenpox: small itchy red spots, fever, and aches and pains. Yes, you've definitely got it. No school for a week, I'm afraid."

"A WEEK?" said Bertie.

Suzy stuck out her tongue and drooped back upstairs to bed.

Dirty Bertie

"What about me?" asked Bertie, pulling up his shirt. "My tummy's a bit blotchy. Do you think that's chickenpox?"

"I think that's dirt," said Mum. "Now finish your breakfast. And keep away from Suzy, chickenpox is very catching."

Bertie sighed. It wasn't fair. How come his sister caught chickenpox when he never got anything? If anyone ought to catch something it was him. He hardly ever washed his hands. Now Suzy would get a whole week off school while he had to sit through boring lessons with Miss Boot. Bertie gulped. He'd just remembered what day it was.

Friday – homework day. As usual Bertie had put off doing his homework until the last minute. Then at the last minute he'd forgotten altogether. Miss Boot, however, would not forget. Anyone who didn't hand in their homework on time risked execution or worse.

Dirty Bertie

If only I had chickenpox, thought Bertie. He felt his head. It did feel a bit hot. He scratched under his arm. He was definitely a bit itchy. The more he thought about it the more he was convinced he was getting it.

"MU-UM!" he wailed. "I don't feel well!"

"There's nothing wrong with you," said Mum. "You just ate two bowls of cereal."

"Yes, but that was before. Now I feel sick!"

"Don't talk nonsense, Bertie. Hurry up and clean your teeth."

Bertie stomped upstairs to the bathroom. How come no one ever believed him? For all they knew he could be dying! He looked in the mirror. *Just my luck*, he thought. *Not a single spot.*

But wait a minute, didn't Mum say chickenpox was catching? Well then he'd just have to catch it. After all, why should his greedy sister keep it all to herself?

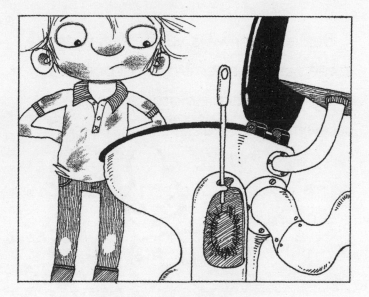

CHAPTER 2

Germs, thought Bertie. That's what he needed. Germs spread diseases – and luckily they were everywhere. His parents were always saying, "Don't touch that, Bertie, it's covered in germs!" Cats and dogs had germs. Toilets were crawling with them. You got germs from picking your nose or eating sweets off the floor.

Dirty Bertie

Bertie had always wanted to examine some germs under a microscope. He imagined tiny armies of them, with scowling faces and hairy legs. Cold germs would be green. Chicken-pox germs would be spotty. But where did you catch them? Bertie looked around and his eye fell on Suzy's pink toothbrush. That would be covered in her germs! He squeezed out a large blob of toothpaste. Cleaning your teeth with your sister's toothbrush was a bit disgusting, even for him, but if it meant missing school it would be worth it.

Dirty Bertie

"Bertie!" called Mum. "What are you doing up there?"

"Nothing!" shouted Bertie. "Just cleaning my teeth."

He swallowed some toothpaste to give the germs a better chance to work. Then he stared at his face in the mirror and waited. Unbelievable – not a single spot! What did you have to do to catch a few measly germs?

On the landing he met Mum carrying a glass of lemonade.

"Is that for Suzy?" asked Bertie. "Can I take it to her?"

"Why?" said Mum, suspiciously.

"I'm just being helpful."

"Hmm," said Mum. "Better not, I don't want you catching her germs."

"I won't!" said Bertie. "I won't even go near her. I'll just put it down where she can reach it."

Mum eyed Bertie strangely. It wasn't like him to offer to help. "OK, but don't spill any. And don't go bothering her!"

Bertie smiled to himself. Once Suzy had drunk from the glass it would be covered in her germs. One little sip of that lemonade and he'd be drinking billions of them.

Dirty Bertie

Suzy was sitting up in bed, looking pale.

"What do you want?" she groaned.

"I brought you some lemonade," said Bertie, smiling sweetly.

Suzy narrowed her eyes. "Why? What are you up to?"

"Nothing," said Bertie. "I'm just looking after you."

"You don't fool me," said Suzy.

"You want to catch my chickenpox so you can stay off school."

"I don't!" lied Bertie. "Have some lemonade!"

"I'm not thirsty."

"Just a sip."

"Go away!"

"Let me help," said Bertie, pressing the glass to Suzy's lips. He tipped it up. Suzy choked and spluttered. Lemonade spilled on her pyjamas and splashed the sheets.

"MUUUM!" wailed Suzy. "BERTIE'S BEING MEAN!"

Mum's feet pounded up the stairs.

"What's going on?" she demanded.

"Nothing!" cried Bertie.

"BERTIE WET THE BED!" howled Suzy.

"Bertie!" shouted Mum. "GET OUT!"

Dirty Bertie

Bertie escaped to his bedroom. He
still had the glass and luckily there was
a little lemonade left in the bottom.
He could almost see the germs swimming
around like tiny tadpoles. *Chickenpox here
I come!* he thought, gulping down the
drink in one go. He ran to the bathroom
and stared at his face. A minute passed.
Two minutes. He inspected his belly. Not
a single spot or blotch. *This is so unfair,*
thought Bertie. Suzy got chickenpox
without even trying!

Time was running out. Any minute
now Mum would drag him off to school
and he would have to face Miss Boot.
There was no escape. Unless … he
suddenly remembered his mum's big

blue medical book. Bertie found
it on the kitchen table. Boils, bruises,
burns ... chickenpox – here it was!

Chickenpox

Illness common in children

Symptoms:
Small itchy red spots,
fever, aches and pains, sickness,
loss of appetite.
(see fig. 1)

Treatment:
Bed rest. If a child has
chickenpox do NOT send
them to school. Even if
they beg you.

fig. 1

Bertie read it twice through then closed the book. *Maybe I don't actually need to catch anything*, he thought. He just had to make Mum *believe* he had chickenpox. Then he'd be safe. No Miss Boot, no school and no handing in smelly homework.

CHAPTER 3

"Bertie, where are you? We need to go!" yelled Mum.

Bertie dragged himself downstairs and slumped into the hall.

"I'm tired," he moaned.

"Don't droop," said Mum. "We're late and I need to get back to Suzy. Now hurry up."

Dirty Bertie

She opened the front door and marched off down the road.

Bertie dawdled behind at a snail's pace.

"Can't you walk a bit faster?" grumbled Mum.

"I'm tired!" moaned Bertie. "My legs hurt!"

"Bertie, stop all this nonsense!" said Mum. "There's nothing wrong with you! Now get a move on!"

"There is!" wailed Bertie. "I've got aches and pains."

"Where?"

"All over," said Bertie.

Mum rolled her eyes. "I don't have time for this, Bertie. You're going to school and that's that."

She strode off down the road. Bertie made I'm-going-to-be-sick noises.

Mum kept walking.

"Blech! Urggle!" Bertie sounded as if he was choking.

Mum spun round. "NOW WHAT?"

"I think I'm going to be sick!"

"So which is it then? Your legs hurt or you're feeling sick?"

"Both," said Bertie. "I think I must be really catching it."

"Catching what?"

Dirty Bertie

"Chickenpox!"

Mum bent down to examine his face. "Chickenpox, eh?" she said. "So where are the spots then? Show me."

Whoops, thought Bertie. He'd completely forgotten about the spots.

Mum folded her arms. "Oh dear, yes, this is serious," she said. "Very serious. I see what you've got. It's *homework-itus*."

"Um, is that bad?" asked Bertie.

"Very bad. You catch it when you don't do your homework. There's only one cure, I'm afraid."

"Staying at home?" asked Bertie, hopefully.

"No," said Mum. "Telling your teacher. I'm sure Miss Boot will know what to do. Come on!"

CHAPTER 4

They reached the school gates. Bertie waved to his friends Darren and Eugene, who were clutching their homework books, ready to hand in. Miss Boot was prowling the playground glaring at anyone who dared to make a noise. Over by the railings Bertie spotted Angela Nicely, sucking on a stick of liquorice.

Dirty Bertie

Angela lived next door to Bertie. She was six years old and madly in love with him. Normally he tried to avoid her, but right now she was his only chance.

"Is that liquorice?" asked Bertie.

"Yes," beamed Angela, proudly. "I bought it with my pocket money."

"Can I have a bit?"

Angela shook her head. "No! It's mine!"

"Go on, just a little bit."

"I already sucked it. It's got my germs!" said Angela, waving the soggy liquorice.

"I'll swap you my apple," said Bertie.

"No thanks."

Dirty Bertie

Bertie didn't have much time. His Mum had finished chatting to Mrs Nicely and was getting ready to go.

"I'll give you fifty pence," he said. "I'll bring it to school on Monday."

Angela considered. She could buy a lot of liquorice with fifty pence.

"Brownie's honour?" she said.

"Yes, yes, Brownie's honour."

Angela took a last suck of the liquorice and handed it over. Bertie popped it swiftly in his mouth and chewed. Mum was coming. "Bye, then, Bertie. Have a good day at school."

Bertie swallowed. "Mmmmnhh!" he groaned.

"What?"

Bertie pointed to his throat. "Mmmmnh! Mmmmnh!" he croaked.

Dirty Bertie

"What? I can't hear what you're saying!"

"My throat hurts!"

Mum sighed heavily. "Bertie, we've been through all this. There's nothing wrong with you."

"There is!"

"OK, show me. Open your mouth."

Bertie opened his mouth and stuck out his tongue.

"GOOD HEAVENS!" shrieked Mum. "IT'S BLACK! WHY DIDN'T YOU SAY SO BEFORE?"

Dirty Bertie

Bertie lay on the sofa and zapped on
the TV. It was going to be a brilliant day.
Suzy felt too sick to leave her bed so
he had the front room all to himself.
He gulped down some lemonade and
slurped up another spoonful of
chocolate ice cream. It had all worked
out perfectly. Mum had wanted to call

the doctor straight away, but by the time they got home his tongue was looking much better. Still, she decided it was best to keep him off school. Bertie smiled to himself as he took another swig of lemonade. He didn't have to face Miss Boot and he hadn't even had to catch any horrible spots.

Dirty Bertie

Next morning, Bertie woke up early. *Brilliant*, he thought. *Saturday!* The sun was shining and he didn't have to go to school. He threw on his clothes and dashed downstairs.

"Oh, you're up," said Mum. "How are you feeling this morning?"

"Much better," said Bertie. "Can I go to the park with Darren and Eugene?"

"Certainly not," said Mum. "I don't want them catching your germs."

Bertie frowned. "I haven't got any germs," he said. "I'm better now. I thought I was catching something, but it turns out I wasn't."

"Really?" said Mum. "Have you looked in the mirror?"

Dirty Bertie

Bertie felt his face. Suddenly he felt itchy. And hot. He dashed into the hall and stared at his reflection in the mirror.

It couldn't be! It was! His face was covered in hundreds of spots!

CHAPTER 1

Bertie loved Sunday afternoons. Gran
often dropped in for tea and brought
one of her yummy home-made cakes.
Today it was Bertie's favourite: Triple
Chocolate Fudge Cake.

"Bertie," said Gran. "What are you
doing next Saturday?"

"Nuffink," replied Bertie with his

mouth full.

"Well how would you like to go dancing with me?"

Bertie choked, spraying cake crumbs all over the table.

"ME?"

"Yes, I'm entering a competition and I'm stuck for a partner. Stan's put his back out mowing the lawn."

"But I can't dance!" said Bertie.

"Of course you can. You've got two feet."

"And you went to the school disco," Mum pointed out.

"I didn't dance!" said Bertie, horrified. "I just ate crisps!"

"Well, I'm sure you'd get the hang of it with a little practice. Please, Bertie. For your gran."

Dirty Bertie

Bertie shook his head. No way was he
going anywhere near a dance floor ...
especially not with Gran. The kind of
dancing she did was the kind he'd seen
on telly. *Ballroom dancing!* It was all
prancing round in tight trousers and
fluffy petticoats. There was no way Gran
was going to talk him into this one! He'd
rather eat dog food than have to dance
like that.

Gran sighed. "Oh well, I'll just have to find someone else to share the prize."

Bertie paused mid-mouthful. "What prize?"

"No never mind, if you're not interested."

"I am! What prize?"

"Well, if we won the contest, the prize is a luxury cruise to New York."

Bertie's eyes boggled. New York! Land of hot dogs and hamburgers! A luxury cruise meant a swimming pool and his own servants. Maybe the captain would even let him steer the boat into New York!

"And would I have to take time off school?" he asked.

"Well if you won, I suppose so," said Mum.

Dirty Bertie

"I'll do it!" declared Bertie.

"YEEE HOOOOO!" yelled Gran, grabbing him by the hands. She whirled him round and round the kitchen, until she got dizzy and collapsed into a chair.

Yikes! thought Bertie. *If this is what she calls dancing, we're in trouble!*

CHAPTER 2

The following evening, Gran dragged
Bertie along to her dance class. He
stared in horror at the couples shuffling
round the hall. Most of them looked
older than Egyptian mummies.

Miss Twist, the teacher, stepped
forward. She was tall and thin as a ruler,
with her hair scraped back into a bun.

Dirty Bertie

"How lovely to see a new member," she trilled. "A special welcome to Bertie!"

The class clapped. Bertie doubted that they'd be clapping once they saw him dance.

Miss Twist divided them into groups to practise their steps. They began with the waltz.

"And step ... step ... slide-together," chanted Miss Twist. "Bertie, glide, not stamp! And stop looking at your feet!"

Dirty Bertie

Bertie groaned. This was impossible. How could he tell what his feet were doing if he couldn't look at them?

"One, two, three. One, two, three," went the class, gliding like swans.

CLUMP! STOMP! STOMP!

CLUMP! STOMP! STOMP! went Bertie, clomping like an elephant.

Things got worse when it was time to dance with Gran. She was twice as tall as Bertie, so he found himself squashed against her chest.

Gran sighed. "You're meant to be leading!"

"How can I lead if I can't see where I'm going?" moaned Bertie.

At last it was time for a break.

"Phew, I'm pooped!" wheezed Gran, mopping her brow. Bertie bought a can of drink and sat down beside her.

They watched a tall, sun-tanned couple practising their steps. The man had hair like Elvis. They whirled across the floor as if they were glued together.

"Good, aren't they?" said Bertie.

Gran rolled her eyes. "That's Keith and Kerry-Anne — South East Champions, as they never fail to mention. They're hot favourites to win on Saturday."

Bertie gaped. "You mean we've got to beat *them*?"

"I'm afraid so."

Keith was stamping and waving his arms as if he was trying to take off.

Dirty Bertie

"What's he doing?" asked Bertie.

"It's called the *paso doble*," Gran explained. "It's like a bullfight."

Bertie's eyes lit up. A bullfight? Now that was *his* kind of dancing. Much better than a drippy old waltz. Bertie imagined he was a famous matador entering the bullring. He swept off his red cape and bowed. The crowd chanted his name: "EL BERTO! EL BERTO! EL…"

"BERTIE!" hissed Gran, prodding him in the ribs.

Bertie looked up to see the South East Champions beaming down at him. Close up, Keith's hair looked like a racoon's bottom.

He patted Bertie on the head. "Hello, little man. Having a good time?"

"I was," scowled Bertie.

Kerry-Anne laid a hand on Gran's arm. "Oh Dotty, so *sorry* to hear about poor old Stan. So you won't have a partner for Saturday! *Isn't* that a shame, Keith?"

Keith yawned. "Yeah, shame. Still, you were never likely to win, were you?"

"Oh, don't worry," said Gran. "I'm not giving up. I've found a new partner, haven't I, Bertie?"

Bertie opened his mouth and let out a burp. Keith and Kerry-Anne burst out laughing.

"HA! HA! Oh that's so SWEET! Your grandson! HA HA!"

Gran folded her arms. "I don't see what's so funny. Bertie happens to be a very talented dancer."

"Yes," said Bertie. "And I've watched it on TV."

Dirty Bertie

"Then you probably know we're the South East Champions – three years running," boasted Keith. "Our *paso doble* is legendary!"

"Huh!" said Bertie. "We're doing the passo doobie, aren't we, Gran?"

Gran's eyebrows nearly hit the ceiling.

"You?" scoffed Keith. "You couldn't dance the hokey-cokey! Come on, Kerry-Anne, let's leave these amateurs to their dreams."

Dirty Bertie

Bertie nudged Gran. "Did you see that? He's wearing a *wig*!"

"Never mind that," groaned Gran. "Why did you tell them we're going to dance the *paso doble*?"

Bertie shrugged. "It just came out. Anyway, I thought you wanted to win?"

"I do. But the *paso doble* takes months of practice!"

Bertie slurped the rest of his drink. "Well then, we better get started."

CHAPTER 3

For the rest of the week Bertie practised every spare minute. He was determined that he and Gran were going to win the contest. No way were creepy Keith and Kerry-Anne winning that luxury cruise.

Bertie threw himself into learning to dance like a matador. He practised his steps in his bedroom, stomping up and

Dirty Bertie

down until his dad yelled at him to be
quiet. He practised on his way to school
– which drew funny looks from people
at the bus stop. And on Friday Mum
found him having a tug-of-war with
Whiffer in the kitchen.

"Bertie! What on earth are you
doing?" she cried.

"Practising!" panted Bertie.

Mum took a closer look. "That's not my best scarf, is it?"

"I've only borrowed it. I need it for my costume."

"It's filthy! Take it out of Whiffer's mouth!"

"I'm trying!" gasped Bertie. "He won't … let … go!"

There was the sound of something ripping. Whiffer let go.

"Phew!" puffed Bertie, sitting down. "Dancing is hard work."

3 1 0

Saturday, the day of the contest, arrived. The finals were at the Regency Ballroom. Bertie's family were coming even though he'd begged them to stay away. Suzy said she wouldn't miss it for the world.

Dirty Bertie

On the way Gran and Bertie called in at the hire shop to pick up their costumes. Gran's dress was Spanish, with bright red polka dots. Unfortunately, it was made for someone a lot smaller than her. Bertie stood outside the changing rooms while she wrestled with the zip.

"You'll have to breathe in," panted the shop assistant.

"I AM breathing in!" moaned Gran.

Bertie had a smart matador's costume with a black hat and a scarlet cape. He stood in front of a tall mirror, swirling the cape like a bullfighter.

Dirty Bertie

"Olé! Olé! Ol-oops!" A stack of boxes toppled off the counter. Quickly he bent down to pick them up. The boxes contained practical jokes such as ice-cube flies and whoopee cushions. Most interesting of all was a small red box.

Bertie's eyes gleamed. Think what you could do with itching powder! You could use it on someone you didn't like – Keith or Kerry-Anne for instance. Come to think of it, that wasn't a bad idea. It might even help him to win the contest.
He slipped the box into his pocket and left some money on the counter.

CHAPTER 4

At the Regency Ballroom the audience were taking their seats. Bertie and Gran hurried backstage to get ready. While Gran pinned up her hair in front of the mirror, Bertie looked around ... now was his chance.

He set off in search of their rivals. He found Kerry-Anne in her private dressing room, wearing a petticoat and a scowl.

"What do you think you're doing?" she snapped.

"Oh, sorry, I was um … looking for Gran," said Bertie.

"She's not here," said Kerry-Anne. "But since you've barged in, you can make yourself useful. Fetch me my dress from the rail. It's the blue one with the sequins."

Bertie closed the door. This was too good a chance to miss. He found the dress on the rail. Checking to see no one was watching, he took out the red box from his pocket.

Keith's laugh boomed from the next room. "HA HA! It's hilarious! The kid hardly comes up to her waist!"

Dirty Bertie

That did it.
Bertie shook
some of the
orange
powder into
the lining of the
dress.
It wouldn't take

long to work – then they would see
who was hilarious.

"Ladies and Gentlemen, will our dancers
please take to the floor for the *paso
doble!*"

The lights dimmed and a trumpet
fanfare split the air. *This is it*, thought Bertie.

His costume was making him sweat.
Worse still, his cape was so long it kept

getting under his feet.

"Bertie, we're on!" whispered Gran, shoving him in the back. Bertie stumbled on to the floor. The audience giggled. They'd never seen a matador wearing plimsolls. Gran skidded into the spotlight, grabbing Bertie to keep her balance.

In the front row, Mum, Dad and Suzy tried to keep a straight face. The music started. Keith, Kerry-Anne and the other couples wove patterns across the floor.

Bertie swirled his red cape round and round. He was El Berto the fearless matador.

STOMP! STOMP! went his feet.

SWISH! SWISH! went his cape.

STOMP!

SWISH! … ARGH! The cape had gone right over his head.

Dirty Bertie

Bertie blundered about blindly, trying to get it off.

"Ow!" He collided with something soft. It was Gran and the two of them wobbled and swayed like wrestlers on ice. Gran stepped on the train of her dress and fell over. Bertie landed on top of her.

"LOOK OUT!" cried one of the couples, but it was too late…

CRAAAAASH!

THUMP!

THUD!

Bertie pulled off the hat which had fallen over his eyes. Dancers lay struggling in a messy heap of arms, legs, bows and ruffles. Bertie clambered off Gran, whose dress had split at the back revealing her winter vest.

Dirty Bertie

A judge was marching towards them
with a clipboard and a grim expression.
Bertie had a feeling his dancing days
were over.

3 1 0

Gran and Bertie sat watching the final
in progress. The judges had disqualified
them as a danger to other contestants.

"Oh well," said Gran. "We did our best. Sorry we won't be going to New York."

"It's OK," shrugged Bertie.

"It's just a pity those two show-offs are going to win," said Gran. "They'll be bragging for weeks. Look at them!"

Bertie watched Keith lift Kerry-Anne over his head. Her shoulders twitched.

"I wouldn't be so sure," he said. "Maybe things are just warming up."

Certainly Kerry-Anne was beginning to act rather strangely. She was wriggling around as if she had ants in her pants.

Down on the dance floor, the itching powder was beginning to work.

"What's wrong with you?" hissed Keith.

"I can't help it!" she moaned. "It's this dress. It's so itchy!"

She clawed at her back.

Dirty Bertie

"Stop doing that!" snapped Keith. "People are staring! Pull yourself together!"

"I'm trying!" squealed Kerry-Anne. "But… Eeek! Argh! Ohh! It itches!"

She stamped her feet and pawed at her arms. She scratched her back like a dog with fleas. Keith tried to grab her hands, but she shook him off.

"DON'T JUST STAND THERE!" she yelled. "DO SOMETHING! I'M ON FIRE!"

Dirty Bertie

Keith did what you do when something is on fire. He snatched a jug of water from the nearest table and emptied it over his partner's head.

There was a brief, terrible silence. Then Kerry-Anne screamed.

"ARGHHH! YOU ... YOU ... IDIOT!"

She swiped at Keith. He gasped and turned bright pink. Clutching at his bald head he fled from the hall.

"See!" shouted Bertie. "I told you it was a wig!"

Dirty Bertie

The audience cheered. If this was ballroom dancing they wanted more.

Gran took off her glasses and wiped her eyes. "Well," she grinned. "That was the best show I've seen in years. I wonder what got into Kerry-Anne?"

Bertie looked blank. "Search me," he said. "Maybe she just had an itch."

Things hadn't worked out so badly in the end. He wouldn't be going to New York, but at least he still had the itching powder. And there was plenty left in the box.

I wonder if Miss Boot can dance? thought Bertie. There was one way to find out.

CHAPTER 1

Mum put down the phone. "That was Gran. She can't come."

"What?" said Dad. "But she's babysitting tonight!"

"She was. But she went to the dentist today and now she's got toothache."

Dad groaned. "What are we going to do? Paul and Penny are expecting us."

Dirty Bertie

Bertie looked up from the comic he was reading. "It's OK," he said. "I can look after myself."

It would be great not having a babysitter. Suzy was sleeping over at Bella's so he would have the house all to himself. He could have a perfect evening: scoffing crisps, watching TV, scoffing chocolate and staying up late. Gran was a hopeless babysitter anyway – she always fell asleep in the middle of playing pirates. And, besides, Bertie didn't see why he needed a babysitter. He wasn't a baby. He knew where the snacks were and how to work the TV, so he could look after himself.

Mum didn't agree.

"Don't be ridiculous, Bertie," she said. "We can't possibly leave you on your own."

Dirty Bertie

"Why not?" asked Bertie.

"What if something happened?"

"Like what?"

"Like you burning down the house," said Dad.

Mum sighed. "I'll just have to ring Penny and cancel."

"We let them down last time," said Dad. "There must be *someone* who could babysit. What about Alice?"

"She's back at college."

"Jackie then?"

"She won't come, not after Bertie put a slug in her hair."

"It wasn't a slug!" protested Bertie. "It was a snail!"

"I know!" said Mum. "What about Kevin?"

Bertie looked up. Kevin? Spotty Kevin from over the road? Were they *mad*? He hardly ever spoke! Bertie thought he'd rather do his homework than spend an evening with Kevin!

"Does Kevin babysit?" asked Dad, doubtfully.

"It's worth a try. I'll ring his mum and find out."

Dirty Bertie

Five minutes later it was all settled. "He's
on his way," announced Mum.

"Oh don't worry about me!" said
Bertie, bitterly. "You just go out and leave
me with Frankenstein. I'm sure I'll be
fine."

"Bertie, he's just a normal teenager,"
said Mum. "I expect he's a bit shy!"

"He doesn't look shy to me," said
Bertie darkly. "He looks like a murderer."

"Anyway it'll be nice having a boy to
babysit for a change," said Mum. "Maybe
he likes playing games?"

Bertie scowled. He hated having
babysitters. And Kevin was going to be
the worst ever.

CHAPTER 2

DING DONG!

Mum hurried to open the door.

"Kevin! How are you?" she trilled. "Bertie's in the lounge. He's so excited you're babysitting!"

Kevin drooped into the lounge.

He looked like he was going to a funeral.

He was wearing black jeans, a black

T-shirt and a long black coat. His T-shirt said "The Dead Skunks" and had a picture of a skull on it. He stared at Bertie through a dark curtain of hair.

"Right, we better be off," said Mum, brightly. "Don't stay up late, Bertie."

"And don't make a mess," added Dad.

They hurried out, slamming the door behind them.

Kevin flopped into a chair. A heavy silence filled the room. Bertie picked his nose. He waited for Kevin to tell him to stop. Kevin just sat there like a dark cloud. Bertie looked at the ceiling and let out a loud burp. He glanced at Kevin. Kevin looked bored to death. Bertie plonked his feet on the coffee table. Kevin scratched one of his spots and examined his finger.

Dirty Bertie

Bertie couldn't understand it. Most
babysitters told him off in the
first five minutes.

He looked around for something to
do next. "I'm hungry," he announced.
Kevin looked at him.
"Usually Mum lets me have a snack
when she goes out. Can I get one?"
Kevin shrugged. "Whatever."

Great! thought Bertie. Normally he had to go on and on for hours before he got a snack — and even then it was one measly biscuit. When Alice babysat she made him eat fruit. But Kevin didn't seem to care what he did.

Bertie stole into the kitchen. He eyed the "Treats" cupboard where Mum kept all the forbidden goodies. He wasn't allowed to snoop in there. Not since the time he'd made himself sick eating a family-size bar of chocolate. Still, one tiny little snack wouldn't hurt, and Mum would never find out. Bertie opened the cupboard and peeped inside.

A door creaked.

Bertie jumped, banging his head and dropping the bag of crisps he was holding. When he looked round Kevin

was leaning in the doorway watching
him. It was creepy
how he could
appear
without
making a
sound.

"Oh, hi,"
said Bertie.
"I was just um
... getting some
crisps."

"Yeah?" said Kevin.

"Do you want some? Crisps?"

Kevin shrugged. "If you want."

"Right. What flavour?" asked Bertie.
"We've got plain, prawn cocktail or
cheese and onion?"

Kevin took all three.

Dirty Bertie

CRUNCH! CRUNCH! CHOMP!

Bertie watched in amazement as Kevin wolfed down the crisps. He chewed with his mouth open. He slurped and burped and dropped bits on the carpet. *And Mum and Dad say I'm a messy eater!* thought Bertie. They'd obviously never seen Kevin.

Dirty Bertie

"Had enough?" asked Bertie.

Kevin dropped the empty bags on the floor.

"We've got biscuits."

"Yeah?" said Kevin.

"In the tin. Or chocolate bars – but Mum notices if they're missing."

"Yeah?"

"Yeah." Bertie thought it over. "I suppose one would be OK," he said.

CHAPTER 3

BUUUUURP!

Bertie lay back on the sofa and patted his full stomach. To tell the truth he felt a bit sick. Kevin wiped chocolate from around his mouth. The room was littered with crisp packets, chocolate bar wrappers and biscuit crumbs. Kevin glanced at the clock.

Dirty Bertie

Uh oh, thought Bertie. It was almost nine o'clock – way past his bedtime.

"Mum usually lets me stay up late on Saturdays," said Bertie.

"Yeah?"

"Yeah, when I've got a babysitter."

Kevin shrugged. "Whatever."

Bertie could hardly believe his luck. He never got to stay up later than nine o'clock – even on Christmas Eve. Maybe if he could keep Kevin occupied he could stay up all night?

"Do you want to play a game?" he asked.

Kevin scratched a spot on his chin. Bertie wondered if he could see anything through all that hair.

"I don't mean a board game," said Bertie. "We could play pirate ships.

Dirty Bertie

Or alien invasion. Or maybe have a
pillow fight?"

Kevin stopped scratching.

WHACK! THUMP!

Bertie whacked Kevin. Kevin thwacked
him back.

They bounced up and down walloping
each other with pillows. *This is fantastic*,
thought Bertie. Mum never let him have
pillow fights or bounce on the sofa. She
said something would get broken.

WHUMP!

Bertie swung his pillow back, knocking
over a lamp. The lamp landed on a vase
of flowers. It wobbled and fell over with
a crash.

"Whoops!" said Bertie.

Dirty Bertie

WHUMP! Kevin's pillow walloped him in the face. It split open, filling the room with clouds of feathers.

THUMP! CLUMP! BIFF! BOFF!

They flopped back on the sofa out of breath.

"Phew," panted Bertie. "That was great. What shall we do now?"

He found the remote and switched on the TV. *This is the life*, thought Bertie. Mum and Dad never let him watch telly this late. And there were so many great programmes he wanted to see. He flicked through the channels. A love story – yuck! A cookery show – boring! A quiz show, adverts, more adverts, a horror film… WAIT! Bertie never got to watch scary films.

"Shall we watch this?" he asked.

"*Night of the Zombies III*. Wicked!" said Kevin. "It's *well* scary."

It turned out that Kevin had seen lots of scary films. It was the first time Bertie had heard him say more than three words.

They switched off the big light and settled down to watch the film.

It was midnight. The moon was out. The people in the house were all asleep. An eerie mist rose off the lake. Bertie sunk deeper and deeper into the sofa. He hugged his pillow.

He hoped there weren't actual zombies in this film.

THUD, THUD, THUD!

Bertie gulped. They were coming.

CRASH! A zombie's hand smashed
through a window.

"YEAARRRRGH!" yelped Bertie, diving
behind the sofa.

He peeped out. *The zombies were in
the house. They walked like robots and had
staring eyes. They were climbing the stairs
to where the people were sleeping...*

Bertie chewed his fist. Why hadn't
anyone warned him scary films were so
… scary? Maybe he should go to bed?
But if he went upstairs he'd never get to
sleep. He would lie there all alone in the
dark. And what if the zombies came to
get him? He peeped through his fingers
at the screen.

What was that? The room was
suddenly dazzled with light. Two bright
eyes beamed through the curtains like
headlights. Wait a moment, they *were*
headlights. A car was pulling into the
drive. Help! This was worse than any
horror film! Mum and Dad were
back already!

CHAPTER 4

Bertie looked around wildly. The house looked like it had been burgled. The floor was a sea of crisp packets, biscuits and sticky chocolate wrappers. There was a wet patch on the carpet and beside it the remains of Mum's best vase. One of the pillows looked like a punctured football. White feathers had

settled on everything like snow. Bertie
felt a wave of panic. If Mum and Dad
saw the house like this he was dead.

He shook Kevin by the arm. "Quick!
They're back!"

"What?"

"Mum and Dad! We've got to tidy up!"

Kevin frowned. "You're blocking the
screen! This is a good bit!"

Bertie couldn't believe it. Was Kevin
just going to sit there and watch the
film? This was a matter of life and death!

A car door slammed. Any minute now
Dad's key would turn in the lock. There
was no time to lose. Bertie flew round
the room like a whirlwind. He hid the
pillows behind the TV. He brushed
feathers under the sofa. He righted the
fallen lamp and mopped the puddle on

the carpet with tissues. What else? What else? Mum's best vase! Bertie got down on his hands and knees and picked up the bits. He grabbed flowers and crisp packets and sticky wrappers.

Dirty Bertie

THUD! THUD! THUD!

They were coming up the path! He rushed into the kitchen with his arms full. Quick, quick, where could he hide the evidence? The fridge! No one would look in there! He yanked open the fridge door and bundled everything inside.

RATTLE, RATTLE!

The key was turning in the lock. Bertie slammed the fridge shut and thumped upstairs in a blur of speed. Just in time! He burst into his room, dived under the covers and lay there panting.

Dirty Bertie

"Kevin! We're back!" called Mum. "Was everything OK?"

Bertie listened with his heart pounding. A few minutes later he heard the front door slam. Kevin had gone. Bertie lay back and breathed a sigh of relief. It was a close thing, but he thought he'd got away with it. Mum and Dad hadn't noticed anything. He stole out of bed and crept on to the landing.

"Such a nice quiet boy," said Mum. "I hope he and Bertie got on all right."

"Well at least he's in bed," said Dad. "And the house is still in one piece. Do you want a bedtime drink?"

Bertie froze. No! How could he have been so stupid? His dad always made hot chocolate at bedtime. Hot chocolate needed milk. And milk was kept in the…

CRASH!
CLATTER!
SMASH!

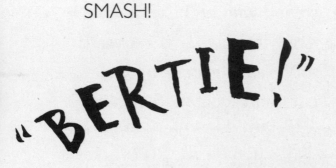

"BERTIE!"